THE DIGITAL DIVIDE
12 THINGS YOU NEED TO KNOW

by Angie Smibert

12 STORY
LIBRARY

www.12StoryLibrary.com

12-Story Library is an imprint of Peterson Publishing Company and Press Room Editions.

Produced for 12-Story Library by Red Line Editorial

Photographs ©: cristovao/Shutterstock Images, cover, 1, 27; Samuel Borges Photography/Shutterstock Images, 4, 21; Meinzahn/iStockphoto, 5; imagedb.com/Shutterstock Images, 6, 28; David Brauchli/AP Images, 7; Riccardo Lennart Niels Mayer/iStockphoto, 9; junpinzon/Shutterstock Images, 10; pcruciatti/Shutterstock Images, 11; Ermolaev Alexander/Shutterstock Images, 12; Piksel/iStockphoto, 13, 29; Lakeview Images/Shutterstock Images, 14; Arek Malang/Shutterstock Images, 15; Andresr/Shutterstock Images, 16; Fuse/Thinkstock, 17; Monkey Business Images/Shutterstock Images, 18; photobyphotoboy/Shutterstock Images, 19; Tero Hakala/Shutterstock Images, 20; Belushi/Shutterstock Images, 22; PathDoc/Shutterstock Images, 23; Michael Jung/iStockphoto, 24; Jevtic/iStockphoto, 25; Martin Mejia/AP Images, 26

ISBN
978-1-63235-224-8 (hardcover)
978-1-63235-250-7 (paperback)
978-1-62143-275-3 (hosted ebook)

Library of Congress Control Number: 2015934329

Printed in the United States of America
Mankato, MN
October, 2015

Go beyond the book. Get free, up-to-date content on this topic at 12StoryLibrary.com.

TABLE OF CONTENTS

What Is the Digital Divide? 4

Why Does the Digital Divide Matter? 6

Who Is Online and Who Is Offline? 8

Why Does Access to the
Internet Differ Worldwide? 10

Who Can Afford Digital Technology? 12

How Does Access Depend on Where You Live? 14

How Is Education a Factor in the Digital Divide? 16

What Is the Primary Language of the Internet? 18

How Do Race and Ethnicity Matter in the Divide? 20

How Do Disabilities Affect Access to the Internet? .. 22

Why Is Age a Factor in the Digital Divide? 24

What Can Be Done to Bridge the Divide? 26

Fact Sheet 28

Glossary 30

For More Information 31

Index 32

About the Author 32

WHAT IS THE DIGITAL DIVIDE?

Technology is a big part of our lives. You can talk, shop, read, play games, and watch movies on your computer or mobile device. You can even go to school online. But not everyone can access or use the Internet. Only 40 percent of the world's people have Internet access. Approximately 4.5 billion

people do not have an Internet connection. This is the simplest definition of the digital divide. It is the gap between those with ready access and those without. Another term for this gap is digital inequality.

Many people cannot afford a computer and high-speed Internet. Others live in rural areas where

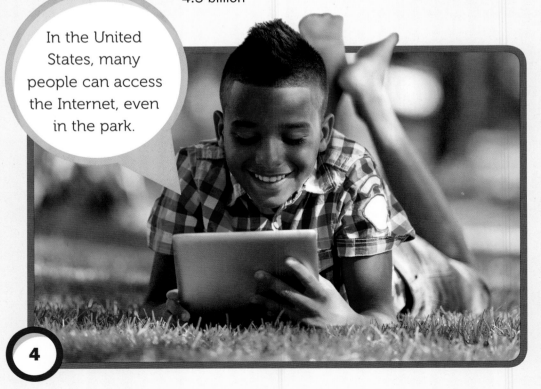

In the United States, many people can access the Internet, even in the park.

Many rural areas do not have access to fast Internet.

fast Internet is not available. Some governments prevent their citizens from using all or part of the Internet. Some people may have limited ability to use the Internet. They lack education, have disabilities, or speak a language other than English. Many people experience a combination of these factors. The digital divide is not just one divide. It's many.

THINK ABOUT IT

What are three possible causes of the digital divide? Reread the text on these two pages to find the causes.

15
Percent of Americans who do not have access to high-speed Internet.

- The digital divide is the gap between those who have ready access to the Internet and those who do not.
- Reasons for digital inequality can include income, education, and age.
- They may also include language, disability, geography, and politics.

WHY DOES THE DIGITAL DIVIDE MATTER?

Information is power. You might use the Internet to watch a movie or play a game. But you can also use it to better your life. People can use the Internet to communicate across long distances. They can make decisions based on news and research they find online. They can make and manage money. Readily accessing the Internet is a huge advantage in many ways.

People who can are considered *information rich*.

People who do not have ready access to the Internet are considered *information poor*. They do not have the same opportunities as those who have ready access. For example, they do not have access to online banking or health news and information. They cannot shop, get

Internet access can give you an advantage in your education and career.

academic help, or search for a job online. They may not be well informed about political issues. When many people in a country lack Internet access, it affects the entire nation. Nelson Mandela was a human rights activist and president of South Africa. He wrote, "eliminating the [difference] between information rich and information poor is also critical to eliminating economic and other inequalities."

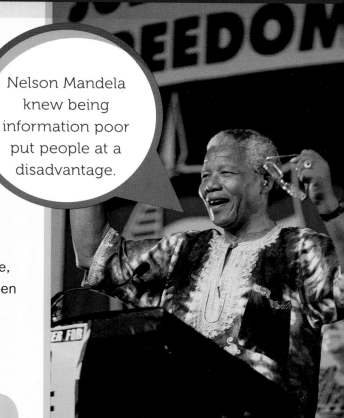

Nelson Mandela knew being information poor put people at a disadvantage.

4 billion

Estimated number of people worldwide expected to be without Internet access by 2017.

- The digital divide determines who has information and who does not.
- People without Internet access have less information, and thus less power and fewer opportunities.
- Lack of Internet access can leave some people behind.

SECOND-LEVEL DIVIDE

Sometimes, most of a country's population has access to technology. But a skill gap may still exist. This is called the second-level divide. The more technical skills you have, the more likely you are to be online. You are more likely to bank and search for a job online. You are more likely to stay informed about government and politics.

7

WHO IS ONLINE AND WHO IS OFFLINE?

Imagine the digital divide as a line running down the middle of a large room. On one side are people with access to high-speed Internet. They are online. These people generally live in developed countries or cities. Many have college educations. They make at least a middle-class income. They speak English. In part because of their Internet access, they are information rich.

On the other side of the room stand the people who are offline. This side is far more crowded. They are more likely to live in rural areas or developing countries. These people earn a lower yearly income. They may have only a high school education. Some have less. Most speak a language other than English. They might be people with disabilities or people over 65 years old. Some may have access to the

GENDER AND THE DIGITAL DIVIDE

By itself, gender is not a barrier to Internet access in many countries. But it may affect Internet use. In the United States, nearly as many women use the Internet as do men. But this is not the case in Morocco in North Africa. There, approximately 62 percent of men use smartphones to access the Internet. Only 38 percent of women do.

Internet. But they do not have the technical skills to use it or to find the information they need. All these people are information poor.

Not everyone who is over 65, uneducated, or low income is offline. Not all people who speak

English and have a college degree are online, either. But people who are offline may face barriers to information that people who are online do not. Some children attend schools without Internet access. They do not have the opportunity to learn the skills they will need to navigate the Internet in the future. This may limit their ability to perform high-tech jobs as adults.

4.2 billion
Number of people in the world without Internet access.

- People with Internet access are most likely to be educated, English speakers, and make a comfortable income.
- Those without access are more likely to be poor, less educated, disabled, elderly, and non-English speakers.
- Internet access helps determine who is information rich and who is information poor.

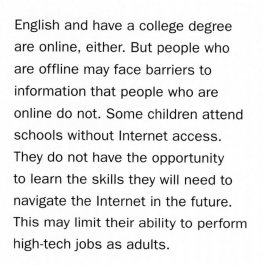

Students in many developing countries do not have Internet access.

WHY DOES ACCESS TO THE INTERNET DIFFER WORLDWIDE?

From 1995 to 2015, the number of Internet users worldwide exploded. It went from approximately 40 million people to 3 billion. People in developed countries are far more likely to be online than those in developing ones. Norway is a developed country. Ninety-six percent of adults there have access to computers, smartphones, or the Internet. Ethiopia is a developing country on the continent of Africa.

Only about 2 percent of Ethiopians have Internet access.

People in developing countries face many barriers to technology access. One barrier is money. Computers can cost hundreds to thousands of dollars. High-speed Internet may cost the same per year. This might not be problem if you live in Norway. The average yearly income there is $40,000 to $50,000. But if you

Many people in developed countries can afford high-speed Internet at home.

Many people in China have Internet access, but the government blocks some websites.

live in Niger, in West Africa, buying a computer might be impossible. The average income there is approximately $430 per year.

Politics can also be a barrier to access. Dozens of national governments restrict or ban Internet access. China, for example, blocks millions of web pages from sources outside the country.

THINK ABOUT IT

Why might someone in a developing country not have access to the Internet? Give at least two reasons.

29

Rank of the United States among countries with the highest percentage of Internet access.

- Developed countries are more likely to have Internet access than developing countries.
- Two reasons for this inequality are income and politics.
- The governments of some countries control access to the Internet.

WHO CAN AFFORD DIGITAL TECHNOLOGY?

The digital divide exists not only between nations but within them. In every country, some people can afford access and others cannot. The more money people make, the more likely they are to have a computer. They are more likely to have access to and use high-speed Internet. In the United States, 85 percent of all adults use the Internet at home, work, or in a public place. Most middle- and upper-income users have fast Internet at home. Two-thirds of low-income families or individuals may have Internet access. But they may not necessarily have access at home. A significant number use the Internet in public

> Most libraries offer Internet access.

SMARTPHONES

Smartphones are changing what it means to be online. Nearly two-thirds of Americans have them. Many low-income adults, especially working-age ones, use smartphones to access the Internet. This is narrowing the digital divide between people of different income levels.

spaces. They may go online at the library or in free Wi-Fi zones. About a third of adults who make less than $20,000 a year are not online at all.

In the United States, $20,000 per year is considered low income. Someone making $1,600 per month struggles to afford a computer and high-speed Internet. Low-income households often spend more than half their income on housing. They seldom have enough money left over each month for fast Internet access.

Smartphones have helped bridge the digital divide.

$300

Monthly cost of the fastest Internet speed available in New York City in 2014.

- In any particular country, some people can afford access while others cannot.
- The vast majority of middle- and upper-income households in the United States have fast Internet at home.
- One-third of low-income families in the United States do not have high-speed Internet at home.

HOW DOES ACCESS DEPEND ON WHERE YOU LIVE?

Where you live may determine whether you have access or not. This is true of developed and developing countries. People in cities are much more likely to have high-speed access than people in rural areas.

Americans in cities are three times more likely to have fast Internet. More than 40 percent of rural schools do not have high-speed Internet. Some rural users might have Internet access, but it might be through a slow or dial-up connection. Remote areas might lack access altogether.

Rural areas typically get services, such as telephone and high-speed Internet, after urban areas do.

Laying cable for Internet is expensive.

Laying the cables for high-speed Internet in rural areas is expensive. Rural areas are more spread out. Internet providers must spend more money to put in cable, DSL (Digital Subscriber Lines), or fiber optic connections. Fewer customers exist in rural areas than in urban areas. Sometimes, high-speed

High-speed Internet makes downloading music faster.

Internet companies are reluctant to provide service because of cost.

15 million

Number of Americans, primarily in rural areas, who do not have access to basic high-speed Internet.

- Rural areas have less access to fast Internet than do urban areas.
- More than 40 percent of schools in rural areas do not have high-speed Internet.
- High-speed Internet costs more for companies to install in rural areas.

HIGH-SPEED INTERNET

In the United States, 78 percent of Internet users have access to at least basic high-speed Internet. This includes cable, fiber, satellite, and DSL Internet services. It is much faster than a dial-up connection. A song that streams instantly over a high-speed connection might take 10 minutes for a dial-up user to download.

HOW IS EDUCATION A FACTOR IN THE DIGITAL DIVIDE?

A large digital divide exists between people with a college education and those without one. In the United States, 96 percent of people with a bachelor's degree or higher own computers. Ninety-one percent of them have high-speed connections. But only 56 percent of Americans with only a high school diploma have computers. Even fewer have high-speed access. This inequality holds true in many other countries. However, the size of the gap varies.

People with more education tend to make more money. With more money, they can buy computers and Internet access. Reading ability and communication skills may also be factors. A person with a high school education or less may have trouble reading and few technology skills. Forty percent of the world population has low reading skills.

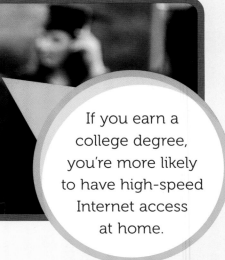

If you earn a college degree, you're more likely to have high-speed Internet access at home.

Not knowing how to use the Internet can be frustrating.

But many websites, including many government sites, are written for someone with a college education. This may discourage some people from using the Internet.

THINK ABOUT IT

What are three possible reasons someone with limited education might not be online? Find your answer in these pages.

37

Percent of Americans with no high school diploma who do not have high-speed access at home.

- A big gap in Internet access exists worldwide between those with a college education and those without one.
- Those with less education tend to make less money.
- They may also lack some technology-use skills.

17

WHAT IS THE PRIMARY LANGUAGE OF THE INTERNET?

Eighty percent of all Internet content is in one of 10 languages. More than half of this content is in English. English speakers make up less than a quarter of the world's people. But they are the majority of Internet users today. Many of the planet's 7 billion non-English-speaking people may not be able to use most websites.

If people do not read English, they might not be able to use most of the information found on the Internet. For example, people in Vietnam may find limited local content in their language. Only 0.5 percent of Internet content is in Vietnamese. Without knowing English, many

If you speak English, you'll be able to read more than half of the content on the Internet.

Vietnamese may not be able to use many international websites. This might discourage people from using the Internet. It might prevent them from learning vital information.

Not speaking one of the Internet's top 10 languages makes it difficult to use the web.

800 million

Average number of English speakers on the Internet in 2013.

- Most of the Internet is written in one of 10 languages.
- Half of the websites in 2015 were in English.
- Not understanding English limits people's access to many websites.

GLOBAL INTERNET

The World Bank keeps statistics on the Internet. The top 10 languages on the Internet are English, Chinese, Spanish, Japanese, Portuguese, German, Arabic, French, Russian, and Korean. These languages account for most of the content on the Internet.

19

9

HOW DO RACE AND ETHNICITY MATTER IN THE DIVIDE?

The countries with the most Internet access are in North America, Europe, and Australia. China, Russia, and parts of the Middle East and South America are not far behind. A digital divide often exists within developed countries. Sometimes, this divide falls between different ethnic groups.

Digital inequality between different ethnic groups is often due to other existing inequalities. In the United

People in low-income areas of a city may not have Internet access while their wealthier neighbors do.

States, digital inequality is rooted in differences in education and economic situations. African Americans, Latinos, American Indians, and Alaska Native communities are more likely to earn less than their white counterparts. They are less likely to have high-speed Internet access in their homes than are white Americans.

But these numbers are changing. In 2014, 74 percent of white households had high-speed Internet. So did 62 percent of African-American households. Fifty-six percent of Latino households had high-speed Internet. This divide narrows as household income goes up. It disappears when comparing smartphone use. Mobile devices are making the Internet more accessible.

Many people access the Internet on smartphones.

22
Percent of Hispanics who access the Internet only through their smartphones.

- The digital divide exists among nations and among different racial and ethnic groups within nations.
- The inequality is often due to other factors, such as education and income.
- Smartphones are narrowing the divide.

21

HOW DO DISABILITIES AFFECT ACCESS TO THE INTERNET?

In the United States, 69 percent of all American adults have high-speed Internet access at home. But only approximately 41 percent of disabled individuals do. People with disabilities often have a harder time using the Internet. It can be difficult to use the web if you are blind. It is also difficult if you have mobility issues, such as paralysis.

Money is one of the main causes of the inequality. Assistive technology is available to help disabled people use computers and the Internet. But this can be expensive. Some people may not be able to afford it. Even if someone can afford the technology, not all websites are designed for it. The Americans with Disabilities Act requires government

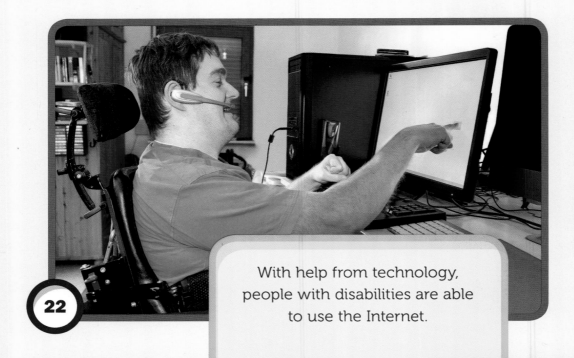

With help from technology, people with disabilities are able to use the Internet.

ASSISTIVE TECHNOLOGY

Assistive technology is also known as adaptive technology. Assistive technology is a term for devices or software that help people with disabilities perform tasks. They include text-to-speech software, special mouse pointers, and closed captioning.

sites to be accessible to persons with disabilities. The European Union has similar standards. However, many sites are still inaccessible or unusable for these users.

For example, a blind person can use software that reads a website's text in an electronic voice. For the text-to-speech software to work, however, the website must be designed correctly. Otherwise, all the user will hear is garbled noise.

Low vision can be a barrier to using the Internet.

WHY IS AGE A FACTOR IN THE DIGITAL DIVIDE?

One side of the digital divide is older than the other. This is called the gray divide. Younger, working adults are much more likely to be online than are senior citizens. Most American adults who are working age have access to the Internet at home or at work. Most of those between 50 and 64 years old are also online. But a little more than half of adults over 65 use the Internet. Fewer than half of them have high-speed access at home. Others choose not to use the Internet at all.

HOW THE INTERNET CAN HELP SENIORS

The Internet can help seniors in many ways. Some health care companies are using the Internet to connect with elderly patients. Doctors may visit seniors on a video conference. Social media and online support groups help seniors stay connected with loved ones. Some thermostats, appliances, and lights can connect to the Internet. Homeowners can control them from a smartphone or tablet.

Some seniors have the skills to use the Internet.

THINK ABOUT IT

Do your grandparents use the Internet? What side of the digital divide are they on? Why do you think this is the case?

47

Percent of US seniors with high-speed Internet access at home.

- Those over 65 years old are less likely to use the Internet.
- They may not believe the Internet is useful to them.
- They may face barriers such as cost, physical limitations, or lack of computer skills.

The gray divide has many causes. Many seniors believe the Internet is not important. They feel they have no reason to use it. Other seniors only use the Internet with someone's help, such as a family member. Some do not know how to use a computer or the Internet. Others cannot use the technology because of a physical limitation, such as loss of sight. The cost of computers and the Internet is also a cause. Many seniors are retired and have lower incomes than younger people do. Others live in rural areas, where access to the Internet is limited.

Sometimes, younger people can help older people get online.

WHAT CAN BE DONE TO BRIDGE THE DIVIDE?

The digital divide is not just one divide. Digital inequality reflects the inequalities that existed in the world before computers were invented. To bridge the digital divide, individuals, organizations, and governments must take different approaches.

Some organizations are working toward making technology more affordable and available to everyone. One such project is One Laptop per Child (OLPC).

Students in Peru use their OLPC laptops.

The organization develops rugged, connected, and inexpensive laptops and tablets. Then, it gives these devices to some of the poorest children in the world. Other organizations send donated computers to developing countries.

Groups and governments are improving high-speed access in rural areas. Still others provide Internet access through libraries and public spaces. Some groups develop training for low-income students and senior citizens. The training teaches participants how to use technology.

All of these efforts arm people with information. They help people become information rich.

$35
Current price for a laptop through the One Laptop per Child program.

- Bridging the digital divide requires many different approaches.
- Some people focus on lowering the cost of the technology.
- Others work to provide training, more public Internet connections, and high-speed Internet to rural areas.

Bridging the digital divide helps all people become information rich.

- The Internet became widespread in the early 1990s. First, those who were tech-savvy were the only ones online. Then, the technology improved. Internet connections became faster. Websites and applications spread across the Internet. More and more people started using it.

- In 1995, US government policy makers began to wonder if access to both computers and the Internet were fairly distributed. The National Telecommunications and Information Administration (NTIA) published a report called "Falling through the Net: A Survey of the 'Have Nots' in Rural and Urban America." The report uncovered a divide between those who had access to technology and those who did not.

- The NTIA found that rural and poor citizens owned fewer computers and had less access to the Internet than did well-off people in cities. Not long after this report was published, the term "digital divide" was coined. During the late 1990s, journalists, educators, politicians, and the public paid a lot of attention to the digital divide.

- By 2010, many of the digital divide gaps started closing. But others may be widening. In 2015, a second-level divide was beginning to take shape. It is between those who have the skills to use computers and the Internet and those who do not.

GLOSSARY

developed country
A country with many industries and relatively few poor people.

developing country
A country with few industries and many poor people who are unable to buy things they need.

dial-up
Slow Internet access in which the computer's modem connects to the Internet over a telephone line.

Digital Subscriber Line (DSL)
A technology for providing high-speed Internet over telephone lines.

fiber (or fiber optic)
A cable consisting of a bundle of glass fibers that carries messages in the form of light.

mobility
Ability to move easily and quickly.

telecommunications
Technology that sends and receives messages over the Internet, phone, and TV.

Wi-Fi
A networking technology that allows computers to connect to the Internet without wires.

FOR MORE INFORMATION

Books

Mason, Paul. *Understanding Computer Safety.* Chicago: Heinemann Library, 2015.

Ohler, Jason B. *Digital Community, Digital Citizen.* Thousand Oaks, CA: Corwin, 2010.

Weinstein, Eric. *Ruby Wizardry: An Introduction to Programming for Kids.* San Francisco: No Starch Press, 2014.

Websites

Code: Studio
studio.code.org

Federal Communications Commission: Kids Zone
www.fcc.gov/kidszone

One Laptop per Child: Map
one.laptop.org/map

INDEX

age, 8, 24–25
Americans with
    Disabilities Act, 22

barriers, 9, 10, 11

China, 11, 20

disabilities, 5, 8, 22–23

education, 5, 8, 16–17,
    21
ethnicity, 20–21

gender, 8
government restrictions,
    10–11

income, 8, 10–11,
    12–13, 21, 27
information poor, 6, 7, 8
information rich, 6, 7, 8,
    27

language, 5, 8, 18–19

Mandela, Nelson, 7

One Laptop per Child
    (OLPC), 26–27

rural Internet access, 4,
    8, 14, 25, 27

second-level digital
    divide, 7
smartphones, 8, 10, 12,
    21, 24

United States, 8, 12, 13,
    15, 16, 21, 22
urban Internet access,
    14–15

About the Author

Angie Smibert is the author of several young adult science fiction novels, short stories, and educational titles. She was also a science writer at NASA's Kennedy Space Center for many years. She received NASA's prestigious Silver Snoopy.